I0648488

John Watson

**Ideals of Strength**

John Watson

**Ideals of Strength**

ISBN/EAN: 9783337101558

Printed in Europe, USA, Canada, Australia, Japan

Cover: Foto ©Andreas Hilbeck / pixelio.de

More available books at **www.hansebooks.com**

# IDEALS OF STRENGTH.

# IDEALS of STRENGTH

BY
### JOHN WATSON
(IAN MACLAREN)

*Author of " Beside the Bonnie Brier Bush," " Home Making," Etc.*

**TOGETHER WITH A SKETCH OF HIS LIFE**

NEW YORK
WILBUR B. KETCHAM
2 COOPER UNION

# JOHN WATSON.

## (IAN MACLAREN.)

---

The Rev. John Watson
M. A., better known as Ian
Maclaren, was born in Mann-
ingtree, Essex, England, in
1850. He is, however, a pure
Scot. It is related that while
yet young the family removed
to London. Some years of his
childhood life were spent at
Perth and Stirling. His parents were decidedly religious,
with strong and positive con-

victions. His father was a faithful elder of the Free Church of Scotland and highly respected. His mother possessed aversions equally strong with her convictions. With a kind spirit that was proverbial, and the record of a life unaffected by class distinctions, and abundant in ministrations to those in trouble, she was lamented at death, and keen was the loss and affection felt for her. Both parents were eminently worthy. Mr. Watson was educated at the University of Edinburgh. He also pursued studies at Tübingen. Among his early school associates were names that have become famous, as Henry Drummond, James Stalker, Robert Louis Stevenson and George Adam Smith. Mr. Watson has said that Scott was the first writer who left any impression on his mind, which author he read eagerly. " Four authors he singles out as masters, Scott, Carlyle, Matthew Arnold and Seely, the author of *Ecce Homo*." He entered the University of the Free Church of Scotland and became assistant pastor of Dr. J. H. Wilson, of the Barclay Church, Edinburgh. A year later he became the minister of the Free Church of Logiealmond, in Perthshire. For two-and-a-half years he remained there.

Perthshire, has been rendered famous, and now well-known as " Drumtochty," to which frequent references are made in his published works. An uncle had been minister there before the " Disruption " in 1843. His literary plans for many years (from the time he was at Logiealmond), were akin to those completed twenty years later. The modesty of Mr. Watson and a natural distrust led to the abandonment, for all these years, of his earlier ideals. Such was his brilliancy and popularity as a preacher, that his fame spread, and invitations came urging him to leave the quiet parish of Logiealmond on the borders

of the Highlands, which was
half Highland and half Low-
land. He accepted an invitation from the St. Matthew's
Church in Glasgow to be col-
league to Dr. Samuel Miller.
Subsequently, three years later, he was called to the Sefton
Park Presbyterian Church,
Liverpool, where he has, with
great acceptability and success,
held its pastorate for seventeen
years. There is no church in
Liverpool, with a larger or
more influential congregation.
Of him Mr. W. Robertson
Nicholl writes and echoes a
universal sentiment, " There
cannot be much hesitation in
saying that among English
preachers of the younger gen-

eration Mr. Watson holds a foremost, if not the first place."

It was upon the appearance of his inimitable work, " Beside the Bonnie Brier Bush," in 1894, that his skill and power in the literary world became famous. The sales of this work in a single year have exceeded 100,000 copies. Mr. Watson was once asked, what suggested to him the picturesque title of his book, —" Beside the Bonnie Brier Bush."

" The title" he replied, " is based on a verse of Scotch poetry, which I have printed on the inner page of the title:

There grows a bonnie brier bush
In our kail-yard.

I meant the title to indicate that as brier bushes grow in humble cottage gardens, so the virtues flourish in very humble lives. A number of people have misunderstood the title. Some like it very much, others disapprove of it. I think, however, they would like it if they understood it."

When asked " what suggested the idea of the book to you ? " he said : " Well, I have always been interested in the study of Scotch character, and used to lecture on it a long time ago, but have not looked at the lectures since. The real reason, however, why I wrote the sketches was that

Dr. Nicholl asked me to do so. That seems rather a bald explanation, but it is the true one. As far as I know, I should never have written them without that request. Of course I could not have written them unless I knew the particular type of life very well."

He has written many works on philosophy and theology. He accepted an invitation to deliver the Lyman-Beecher Lectures to the theological students of Yale, at New Haven in 1896. The Lectures have been published and are full of pertinent and wholesome truths. He also lectured in the principal cities of the

United States, being intensely popular.

Of Mr. Watson's appearance Dr. J. M. Buckley writes, " He appears like a man in full vigor, accustomed to the open air, to considerable exercise and when dressed for travel has an unclerical though not an anticlerical aspect. On the platform, however, he resembles the modern type of the English dissenting minister of the Calvinistic denominations. His voice is of the more ancient ministerial type, approximating a drawl, the upward inflection with a tendency to the minor key and a pronounced rhythm."

His apt descriptions, his

pathetic recitals, his tender utterances, assert his power to the unbiased critic.

He has been surprised at the famous effect his stories have wrought and is full of delight and appreciation that such marked approbation has been accorded him for them. Mr. Watson as preacher, expositor, novelist and lecturer, stands as one of superior power and rare qualities. In all these varied parts and gifts he is a man of distinguished ability. It was indicative of the character of the man that he should still have retained his picturesque *nom deplume* on the title-page of his book, instead of announcing it as the work of Rev. John Watson, the name by which his friends best know him. Concerning his *nom deplume* it may be said that " *Ian* " is Scottish for John, his own name, and the " *Maclaren* " was his mother's name which he thus memorializes. On making an address in Brooklyn, Mr. Watson made some remarks with reference to the pronunciation of the name " *Ian.*" " I would say," he remarked, " that if you want to pronounce it like an Englishman you will say I-an, if like a Scotchman Ee-an, and if like a Highlander Ee-on."

Mr. Watson is ever busy, a very energetic worker, " he

never loiters, he never trifles,
but has always everything in
strict order."

Such are a few of the many
facts in the life peculiarities of
one whose works are of exalted
merit, whose efforts will be
recorded among the noble,
whose name will be heralded
as one of the worthies—an
immortal name that is not
born to die.

# THE FOLLY OF STIFLING RELIGIOUS CONVICTIONS.

"Quench not the Spirit." 1 Thessalonians 5 : 19.

# THE FOLLY OF STIFLING RELIGIOUS CONVIC-
# TIONS.

---

Accurate scholars point out with perfect truth that when St. Paul gave the solemn warning " quench not the Spirit " to the Christians at Thessalonica, he was not referring, in the first instance, so much to religious convictions as to spiritual gifts. Those were days when the Spirit of Almighty God burned like a fire in the bones of men, and when they spoke because they were not able to be silent. Proph-

ets arose in the little Christian
communities, who felt as if
they had a message to the
world, and, come what might,
must deliver it. The Apostle
was anxious that these deliv-
erances of humble prophets
should not be ignored or de-
spised. No doubt they might
speak when they ought rather
to have been silent: they
might also sometimes say
things not worth the saying,
but the Apostle thought it was
better to bear the burden of
too much hearing rather than
to risk the loss of some proph-
ecies. You must take so
much quartz in order to ex-
tract the few grains of gold,
and the man who listened

would be recompensed for much speaking by occasionally a beautiful gleam of divine revelation. The Spirit of God does dwell in a believing and clean heart, the oracle within the heart of a believing man does sometimes stir and move him to speak, and the thing which he then says is a message to his day and generation from one who is living in the fellowship of God. It is a poor little tape that struggles down from the electric machine, but yet upon that tape, in strange and jagged characters, is the message that has flashed from a remote corner of the world. And so these uncultured men gave out, sometimes, their words in rude and ungrammatical speech, but yet it was some-thing they had to say to men's hearts.

What the Apostle says about this has a wide range. If, through worldly indifference and intellectual scorn, we de-spise the revelation that comes by unlearned lips to us, then we have done our best to quench the Spirit of God. But what the Apostle says has a very much more sacred ap-plication, from which none of us can escape, and which I desire to impress upon your lives. The Spirit of God did not simply rest upon the prophets and Apostles so that

they opened their mouths and
spake the will of God. The
almighty and merciful Spirit
of God has had a vaster and
more extended sphere, since
there was a human race on
earth; and through the check-
ered history of humanity, that
Spirit has been striving with
human hearts, and is struggling and striving in our
hearts to-day, however care-
less and thoughtless.

What I mean is the one un-
wearied and Divine influence
has been inside our hearts ever
since we were born, restraining
us from irrevocable excesses
of sin, reinforcing the spiritual
instincts of the heart when
they were heavy and dull,

sustaining the solitary voice of conscience, awakening within us at different times pathetic memories of the Father's house, and giving us what is the sweetest and holiest desires we shall ever have—the desire to return to our Father's love.

Sometime, on an evening, we have stood and looked at the midnight sky, and as we saw the moon and the stars we have thought they also shone upon our fathers. And our fathers' eyes looked upon them, and so in the heart of our fathers moved the same influence that is moving now in ours, in childhood, in manhood, and so on to old age, and

which we may well pray may
never forsake our hearts. It
is unfortunate that most of us
are so unconscious of the most
profound and spiritual facts;
and that perhaps few of us
have ever realized that God
has been within us, and moving us to our salvation. We
have thought of Him as wait-
ing for us in His heaven; we
have thought of Him as coming down in the mission of Jesus, His Son, to get into touch
with human souls. We have
thought of him as speaking by
the blessed Gospels, and His
voice as pouring within our
ears a truth far deeper and
truer than we understood.
That great figure in the Rev-

elation where the Almighty is represented as standing at the door of the human heart and knocking—how true, how anxious, how wistful, how patient!

We have understood that if our hands be but stretched out to the latch, and the latch, by the human will be lifted, and there be but an inch of room, that the grace of God should come in, to our repentance and faith. How true! But have we ever said to ourselves, "He that is without has also been within?" It is so difficult to our minds to imagine the unspeakable love of the Almighty. All you can do is to take one facet of the gem and

look at it, and then turn it to
another; take one figure, drop
it, and then go to another. It
is true that the Father waits
until the son bethinks himself
and returns. But it is also
true He pursues him into the
far country, and makes it mis-
erable there. And more than
that, the Eternal love stirs in
the heart of man as the Spirit
brooding on the black and
sullen waters, bringing out
before his eyes the sight of the
old homestead, the expression
of his Father's face, the motion
of happy servants that come
and go where there is enough
to spare; till at last he brings
the resolution to the birth and
says: "I will arise and go

to my Father." And the God that receives him was the God that moved him.

I do venture to think that within your hearts you have sometimes felt this, one way or another. You have been, for instance, shocked out of your sense of perfection. You have had your habit of self-confidence broken. You have seen the stains of your soul just look black before sinking out of sight. You have been penitent and ashamed, longing to be forgiven and cleansed. Do you know anyone just like that? Or, death came unawares, and took away one that was young. You saw the still and calm face; felt that moment as if you were lying there; you imagined yourself in another world and said: "How shall it be with my soul?" And then your heart failed in you, and you were inclined to kneel and say, "Bless me, even me also, O my Father." Your life lost its freshness and its greenness; pleasures had not their relish, blessings had not their attraction, you were desolate for want of a sight of the Lord Jesus, insulted, scourged, crucified, dying for sins that were not His own. And of a sudden, as by the touch of an enchanter's wand, kindled springs of healing in your heart, and you felt yourself drawn, as the magnet draws, to the cross of Christ. One way or another, some way, it does not matter which, what was it? Did you say a Preacher? Did you say a " Sermon?" Did you say " a fancy?" Did you talk it away? Did you laugh it off? Did you never guess that all this was the love of the Almighty moving within your heart? O beautiful thought, that God should have been within us, and left within us the signs of His presence. I mean you, the person that has felt it. Do you not think so? I seem as if I am in contact now with single human souls. You did not think so: you said it was not

beautiful, you said you would
rather not have had it. Before, you were contented, satis-
fied ; you did all you wanted,
you had rather that you had
been left alone; you would
rather be as you were before.
Do you say so ? I answer,
all merciful the disturbance of
the human life, all merciful
the misery of a human heart ;
and I say that in trying to
overcome this motion of the
Divine love within the depths
of your being, you are engaged
in a vain and fruitless task.
You do not know how much
you have lost, you have no
conception how much you are
loved. You do not know the
patience of the Almighty.

You do not know the exuber-
ant energy of the Divine
Spirit. What a love, to cling
to us and to refuse to let us go!
What a love that has stood out
all our resistance! It has been
like this. Have you ever seen
a young child in its nurse's
arms? Why, when the child
was tired and sleepy, would it
not lie down and sleep? I am
sure no person can tell. But
what it did was to fling itself
back, and refuse to rest. And
the nurse let it sob, held it
firmly, till at last it rested.
Why, it might have rested
sooner! And so it is with this
soul of yours.

We cannot overcome the
persuasion and the resistance

of the Divine love. All this struggling in your souls is only the wrestling against the very arms of love, that will hold you, I hope, unto your salvation. When you try to persuade a person that the Divine Love will receive him, however unloving, and that the Divine pity will rest on him however unworthy,—oh, I have been thankful I have been a poor physician of human souls. There are many ways of giving to a human spirit the healing balm of God's salvation. You can, for instance, say that God is love, and that righteousness and power and wisdom and judgment are all fused and

harmonized in love. You can
point to the mission of the
Lord Jesus, and say that Gali-
lee and Gethsemane and Cal-
vary and the Resurrection are
all the Gospel of love. You
can ask the man whether, in
his own love, he has not had
a mighty and merciful provi-
dence which raised him up
and hedged him from sin.
And all these ways point
him to the heavenly kingdom.
But I do think this is a mere
conventional argument to any
person who is afraid of his re-
ception at the hands of the
Almighty. How is it that
you wanted to return? Why
did you want to be forgiven,
to be cleansed, to be loved, to

be friends with God? Now,
are there not men and women
here that would give much to
be friends with God? We
say, whenever any extraordi-
nary thought crosses our
mind, " That is remarkable,
that did not come from me, I
was unconscious of it: I was
for the moment inspired."
Whenever that want is in the
human heart, I say, " Here is
a prophecy of the kingdom of
the Almighty." Here is the
evangel of his love. It is just
the spirit smiting the hard
heart till it turns into a well
of water. Now let me speak
to this individual. Have you
never been perplexed and dis-
mayed by the commotion in

your heart? Have you been dimly conscious it was God? And then have you felt you would wish to free yourself from the restraining influence, just that you might be as before, just that you might have the old peace? Have you ever done this in the days of old? When you were children, as you went along through the park, has your eye been attracted by a tiny jet of water springing up among the green grass? You said, "It is a spring." And then because you had nothing to do in those happy days, you said, "I will cover it up, and keep the spring down." You have gathered leaves, and earth and stones and built a compact house and said : " No more water from that poor spring will ever get out of that prison." By and by the earth loosened and fell and crumbled away before the irresistible stream of gentle water. It is impossible to restrain the power of nature, and almost impossible to restrain the love of God. I wish I could say, for my own sake and yours, that I could say, entirely impossible. I cannot tell with what longing of heart I wish to believe that no human heart can resist the love of the Almighty; but I have before me the facts of human life. I have before me its ex-

periences. It appears to me
that we have the power of re-
sisting the Divine love, a
power that is perfectly awful.
How do I know? Because
people have done it. Because
sitting in the pews here to-day
there are people who have
done it. You have been able
to forget the voice of God.
You have been able to loosen
that affectionate pressure of
the Divine hand, you have
been able to obliterate the
agitation of the Divine love.
You are to-day as much engaged with business, and as
entirely hopeful, your pleasure is the same to you as it
was before that moment when

God was stirring you. You have got relief.

There are victories that are worse than ten defeats, victories that with clearer eyes we shall regard with vain regret. " Oh to be free from the anxieties and longings of the soul that are despicable! I was never in such a state before, and the sooner it is ended the better. Oh to be free from the pain of a sick soul! I tell you there is something worse than pain, and that is the absence of pain. Just now, as you said, " When will it end? For this is as unreal to me as anything I ever heard." Have you ever thought that the absence of it is worse? When a man lying on his bed is racked in agony we pity, and we stand by his side, and take his hand, and say " We hope you may have strength to be patient." It is far more pitiable next morning when we come, and he says, " This morning, suddenly the pain disappeared, and I am now quite well." Quite well, with the sunken circle beneath the eye, and death's pale ensigns upon his cheek. That is the most pitiable of all. Outside the door, when the door is closed upon him, we look at the physician, and he shakes his head.

" Yes, mortification has set in." We thought so. It

was the beginning of the
end.

Oh! the absence of religious conviction is the most awful thing in human history.
It is the insensibility of the
soul. We are capable—take
this in, and carry it away with
you now—capable of spiritual
suicide. It is given to us to
refuse the Spirit of God or to
yield to it.

I say it again, it is a hard
task. No words can describe
how the Spirit of God can en-
dure rebuff, refusal, insult,
outrage, and cling to a human
heart as a mother clings to a
prodigal son. If He leaves
He leaves because He cannot
stay : if He leaves, He leaves

because He wishes to re-
turn.

The Eternal Love is ever
the same. I never preached
otherwise, I hope I never shall.
But the power of responding
may die from out your soul.
There is to each of us given,
as I take it, a capacity for religious feeling : a capacity for
faith, for repentance, for love.
We can squander it by wilful
neglect and wanton reasoning.
You say then the Spirit of God
is quenched. Yes, but what
does it mean ? It means that
your own spirit, the only power
that can respond to it, is
quenched within you. You
have destroyed it, and it is over.
Now it is peace.

You will not think about this when you leave the subject, not once ; it will have no more effect upon you than a zephyr. When the wood is green, you put it into the fire, and it burns. You take up the charred branch after that, but you can never light it again. Abandoned of the Almighty ! But how ? With his love just breaking over you, in the sadness of utter despair.

" Beyond me," you say, because you do not know it, you are unconscious of it. Years ago on a summer afternoon, I stood on a little harbor wall and saw two vessels trying to make the entrance. They were lying in a narrow chan-

nel, and, since there was not
water enough to keep them up,
they were lying on their side.
But far out the tide began to
turn, and one wave after another passed under them, and
every wave in the channel
the water deeper, and I saw in
a little while that the water
was twelve feet deep in the
harbor, and the green, foam-
ing waves rushed in like a
mill-race. I looked again to-
ward the narrow passage, and
saw on one vessel that they
had taken advantage of the
wind at the right moment, and
on that first vessel they floated
in on the full tide. Upon the
other vessel they were not on
the alert, though sailors do not

often make that mistake, and when they tried to make the harbor the tide had turned, and they could not. The water grew shallower, they gave up the attempt, and gradually the vessel heeled over, and lay just as before on the bank of sand. At nightfall I went down a-gain, and in the dark gloaming I saw the forsaken vessel, and I prayed that I might not miss the tide which God gives to our souls, nor quench His Spirit within my heart.

# THE DECEITFULNESS OF SIN.

"Exhort one another daily, while it is called To-day : lest any of you be hardened through the deceitfulness of sin." Heb. 3 : 13.

# THE DECEITFULNESS OF SIN.

---

There are phrases which light up a subject as a flash of lightning does a darkened country, and embody, as in a a word, what we cannot reveal with much speaking, and one of these happy strokes is this, " the deceitfulness of sin." Sin, as most of us have found, is not only most masterful and dangerous, most disgraceful and degrading, but also most cunning and insidious.

It lies in wait for us at shady corners of our life, and garottes us before we have the chance of resistance or any possibility of escape. It dogs us with stealthy tread, like the step of a Red Indian, it hides itself behind familiar and innocent circumstances, it allures us from the solid pathway of virtue with all kinds of devices, and then, like a will-o'-the-wisp, plunges us into the morass. It holds out to our too eager appetite various excellences, and then afterwards fills our mouth with the apples of Sodom. What I mean is this : I never feel as if I had a chance all my life of a fair, stand-up battle with

any sin. Sin has always
taken men at a disadvantage.
We are perpetually being led
into traps, and overtaken by
surprises, and baffled in various ways. Our strong points,
I appeal to any of you who
ever studied our spiritual
powers, are continually dis-
counted and outgeneralled,
our weaknesses are noticed
and undermined. Every day
I live the conviction comes
more strongly to my mind—
although I cannot in any way
explain it—that behind all
these stratagems and these
temptations that come and go
with an awful sensibleness
and appearance of cunning,
there must be one Personal

Power and one Evil Intelligence with whom I am fearfully and blindly wrestling for the holiness of my life and the safety of my soul.

It would, perhaps, be impossible for any of us to agree upon a particular sin as most dangerous, but I may say there cannot be two opinions about the sin, of all the masterful and deadly sins, which is most insidious, and has the most cunning approaches, although in the end its results be awful and disastrous. You see, there are sins which just fairly grip you of a sudden, you have a hand-to-hand tussle and the result is crowned victor or a disgraced victim.

I could mention such a sin;
it is not necessary. But intemperance very rarely takes
hold of a man like that. If intemperance ever does, it is because the man's father drank,
and the alcoholic taint is in his
veins, and then he falls quite
suddenly, or because he is
placed to a peculiar disadvantage. Peculiarly intemperance
comes with masked and un-
suspected beginnings, and if
you afterwards said to a man,
" Where did you begin ? " he
would not be able to identify
the start. Young children
full of the excitement and heat
of animal spirits, are offered
wine when they are too young
to resist. I do not care to be

dogmatic in this place about the various circumstances of social life, but at once I shall go the length of saying that to give children wine is something approaching a dastardly sin. Women with fine sensibilities and highly-strung temperaments are ordered stimulants during critical circumstances of their lives, and they acquire a habit which, in the end, becomes their master. Young men serve their time in offices where the principals are not so careful as they should be about this thing, and where other young men go out two or three times a day to the bar, and they begin to go also. Bargains are made

in some lines of business, over
refreshments, which could not
otherwise be made, or would
not be made, as one has told
me, at such a profit. And so
the man gets his present profit
and lays the foundation of his
future moral wreck. Gentle-
men take wine without reserve
at dinner; some of whom are
old enough to know better,
some of whom are too young
ever to have begun, others are
not content with a legitimate
use at meal-times, but must
go to a restaurant during the
day for pleasure or for business. I believe that number
is growing smaller, I believe
the day is coming when the
finger of scorn will be pointed

at a man who will go out from
his place for no other purpose
than that of drinking. Now,
mark you, I am not saying a
word just now in regard to intemperance. I am pointing
out boldly how innocent and
moderate drinking prepares
the way. The enemy comes
to us under the form of business relationships and good
fellowship, and with all the
innocent and familiar circumstances of life. We take him
by the hand, for he wears at
that time a pleasant face. We
domesticate him in our life
and home, and afterward find
ourselves in the grip of a tiger.
It is the secrecy of his first ap-
proach, it is the gentleness of

the descent I am now wishing
to drive home on the minds
of those who are still young
people, and also on others.
If you see an old acquaintance,
and an early and honored one,
disgracing himself in the face
of society, then, for the sake
of charity, and for the sake of
your own safety, remember
this—he, perhaps, learned it
first from you and me. And
now suppose the two of you
could go back on the path together, you could not tell the
spot where the two roads di-
verged and where one took the
fatal turn.

You cannot help noticing
that although this sin is not
fastidious about its victims,

and will take the lowest and coarsest, like the prowling tiger, it has won the most un-expected successes with high and gentle spirits. It is not those who are repulsive and unloved that have fallen most ready victims to intemperance. Some of the meanest wretches that walk the streets, whatever may be their follies, seem to be proof against this tempta-tion. No; it is men who are lovable—and men whom we have loved, who have had high instincts, and have had noble hearts, who would not do a person a bad turn, who have many beautiful accomplish-ments. Taking advantage as I argue, and believe to be the

case, taking advantage of their
facile good-nature, of their genial popularity, of their very
heartiness, this sin stalks them
to the death, just as a noble animal of the chase is marked out
through his very beauty, by the
marksmen on every side. You
must know some friend of
yours to whom this happened.
You loved him, and everybody
loved him. Well, when he fell
how sorry we were, we would
rather have seen twelve other
men fall than that man. We
gave him his chance, we ral-
lied around him. He was re-
stored, he fell again—he fell
again—he fell again ; till the
handsome face lost the stamp
of its nobility, and the bright

and refined nature grew fleshly
and coarse.    Yet to the end his
heart was so kind that it would
respond to the merest touch
of friendship, and he had mo-
ments of self-reproach which
were almost an atonement.
We said of him, as our hearts
bled, " he was his own worst
enemy."

Perhaps, you now think,
some of you, that I have fairly
launched on the sea of temperance speaking.  You say,
"I know plenty of men who
are tolerably free livers, and
are robust in health."  Will
you now let me state my point
definitely ?  I am not here to
say there is no alternative be-
tween a man being an absolute

abstainer and a downright drunkard. I am not here to say that because a man uses this thing carefully he will certainly be in more danger than if he did not use it at all, any more than a man who swims is more likely to be drowned than a man who of his own free will never leaves the dry land. I want to make a protest, which I think I may utter, against those rash statements, such as that a moderate drinker is a greater pest, and a more dangerous man, than an absolute drunkard. He is not so physically, he is not so morally, he is not so socially. It is simply sheer nonsense. May I hope now, finally, that we have done with it? But my point is this, that if a man leaves the path of a most conscientious and steady moderation, there is no saying that he may not speedily land in the depths. " I know men who could not be called moderate, in any pulpit sense, and to-day they are not ruined." This you may say, and I ask, how old are they? " About forty," you say. Yes: your case is too young yet, it is just in process. Just now that man has business cares, he has to make his fortune, he has great responsibilities, he is restrained and coerced by the circumstances of life. Give him twenty years of free living, will his will be as clear then, when he is sixty? When he has made his fortune, he is free from business. I would give nothing for him then, when, with a relaxed discipline, as an old man he strips and enters the arena. Ah! this is the testing point. Pitiable that he should break down when he is old and should have been preparing himself to break down for twenty years, when you were standing round and saying how safe he is.

I will take an illustration from another city for obvious, reasons, and I do not think the case can be identified here. If it is, alas! it does not matter. When I lived in that city one of the great professions was conspicuously headed by a man of the most remarkable ability and distinguished fame. His name and position were so great that he could command all the important business that fell within his province, and all that he did, he did most earnestly. He was a leading member of the Scottish church, he was a darling in society, he was a great collector of rare books. All the time habits of excess were eating into the moral and intellectual being of the man, and while outwardly the trunk stood, it was entirely rotten within. Years ago he had to come down from the position he so nobly filled, he was ignored and passed by in the work he used to be the only one to do, and when last I heard of him, that once most honored and conspicious name was covered with obscurity.

Young and strong, but by and by you will be old. How do you know that what you can do just now in this way, you shall be able to do with absolute safety afterwards? You are simply domesticating a tiger-cub, and now you play with it and show it tricks, by and by it will turn and rend you. The one reason, friends, why we have to guard against this sin with such extraordi-

5

nary care, is the fact that it, of all sins, insinuates itself into the fibre of the nature. And immediately it begins to affect the character. Do not think of it as a robe that may have been slipped over you, and when it grows uncomfortable you will fling it off. It is a garment like that Hercules wore, it is soaked in every thread and fibre with poison, and the poison will soon begin to go into your system. What I mean is this, it does not matter how honorable and straightforward a gentleman is before he falls beneath the power of this vice. You are as simple as a child if you expect that in a year after, in that man, the very elements of virtue or of strength will remain. You know that is true, you know that there are men whose foreheads would once have mantled with a genuine blush if charged with falsehood, they would deny a fact now and look into your eye. And you know that that man will condescend to the low, despicable cunning of a savage, no ingenuity has ever been discovered short of absolute confinement that will restrain that man from ruining himself, and he will practise any amount of deceit to obtain the poison which is his destruction.

His character begins just

simply to crumble away like the foundation of a house when the water is running beneath it. I am putting a question to you. Is it not a certainty—I never knew an exception, never—that you cannot depend upon the word of a man who has fallen under the power of this vice! Friends, it is now the victim's will that is to blame. You just look back over your life and try to see if my words are not true. I will give you this little bit of personal history, although I am bound to say it can be no new thing to you, your own memory will be awakened by it, unless your family and friends have been different from every other man's society. One of my few early friends was the son of a good man who held a high position. That boy is now a tramp and a vagabond upon the face of the earth. And if he is living, he will sooner or later come to my house, for he comes to the house of all his old friends, just to get bread. He will go away again, and I tell you his case is hopeless. Give him a little bread, a few clothes, he goes away on the weary track again. At the old Scotch grammar school where I was preparing for the university, we fought like Scottish lads, hardly, for our honors. I struggled for the second place; a lad bright in intellect as he was strong of body, could easily have taken it, but by kind good nature he allowed me to share the second place with him. We went together to the University, both of us studied for the church. In two years he left and went away, although of course we expected his career to be very brilliant. The gayety of the University had proved too much for him. I had a private tutor. He not only drilled me in my Latin composition, but he was one of the first men that gave me a love of letters. He was kindness itself to me, and I loved him. By and by he received a parish. He used to preach ably and effectively, and became very popular. He is not in that parish now, he is not in the church now.

One of my college professors was a man of genial disposition, and a splendid student, but the same enemy was too much for him. He was a good and sincere man, and an able theologian. He does not hold the chair now, he is not in this country. I see them one by one pass to oblivion, with a cloud upon their names.

I apologise. I would not have given a chapter of personal history, were it not that you have, many of you, read it at one time or another.

Your own friends, your boy intimates at school, your fellow clerks—where are they all now? How many of them are living? How many are dead? What did they die of? Clerks that used to be in your first office, your old partner, the man you met in your business,—are there none of their names that occur to you now?

This sin comes into a house like a serpent. We can keep out any other sin, not this one. Your child, the little fellow that used to sit beside you, who used to nestle against you in the church. You see his face to-night; do you know where he is? He whom you loved, now an outcast. You are silent.

What do you propose to do to counteract and destroy this terrible thing, the evil that is eating out the life of the middle class. I say nothing of other classes. Have you any plan? Oh, you must have some plan —you must have some. What do you propose to do to save your children from the power of this vice? How do you propose to save your friend? Are you just going to let him slip? How do you propose to save yourself? I do not think any one plan will do ; I believe you will have to try one, or two or three plans. It is worth all your thought, all your trouble, all your pain. If you could rescue one single man or woman, although it is just about hopeless, rescue them. Try. If you could rescue one man or woman, it would be the greatest achievement of your life. Are you going to fight this evil for yourself? Is there a man here who has to fight it for himself? Then let me say, do not depend on your strength, for this is the deadliest enemy any human being ever had to face.

Young men, will you begin to reason? For I am terrified when I see a young man who does not reason, and, with a blinded, darkened vision, goes as thousands before him have

gone. I seem to see him under the hand of the destroyer.
I know a few men who have
been arrested upon their
course, and turned to glorify
the power of God's name.
Take care where you go, and
with whom. There are sights
in every city that would ruin
an angel if possible. There
are men who have been dragged down before my eyes. I
saw them dragged, and could
not see what hand was below
the water, and I asked for the
cause. It was their "set"
which ruined them. I understood it then. And above all
things, remember this—Christ
nailed the serpent head of
every sin to His own Cross,

and He lives to-day to help
every man and woman to be
delivered from sin, and to give
them final victory.

www.ingramcontent.com/pod-product-compliance
Lightning Source LLC
Chambersburg PA
CBHW030010030726
47499CB00008B/2981